ELISHA COOPER

Magic Thinks Big

Greenwillow Books, *An Imprint of HarperCollinsPublishers*

Magic Thinks Big
Copyright © 2004 by Elisha Cooper
All rights reserved. Manufactured in China
by South China Printing Company Ltd.
www.harperchildrens.com

Watercolors and pencil were used to prepare the full-color art.
The text type is Americana.

Library of Congress Cataloging-in-Publication Data

Cooper, Elisha.
Magic thinks big / by Elisha Cooper.
  p. cm.
"Greenwillow Books."
Summary: A cat sits in the doorway and tries to decide whether to go
inside where he might get fed again, go outside where he might have
an adventure, or stay where he is.
ISBN 0-06-058164-6 (trade). ISBN 0-06-058165-4 (lib. bdg.)
[1. Cats—Fiction.] I. Title.
PZ7.C784737Mag 2004 [E]—dc21 2003012566

First Edition 10 9 8 7 6 5 4 3 2 1

 Greenwillow Books

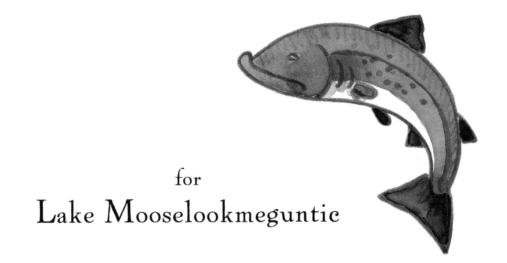

for
Lake Mooselookmeguntic

Magic contemplates his next move.
Should he go in?

Or out?

Or should he stay
right where he is.

If he goes in maybe
he can convince them
to feed him again,

or he could look
inside the fridge,

or wait in front
of the mouse hole.

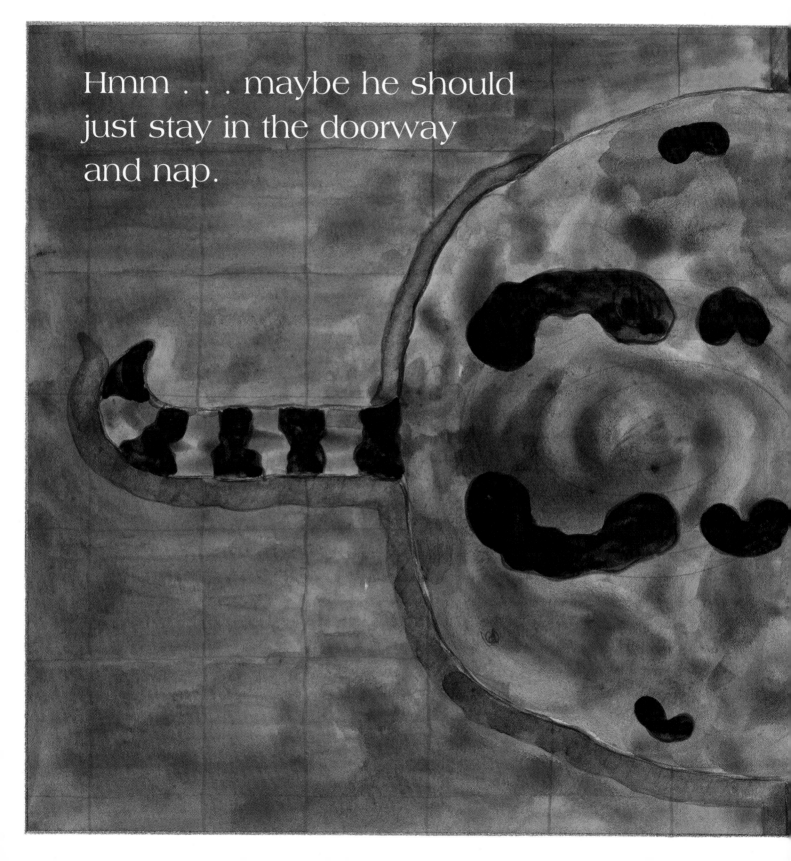

Hmm . . . maybe he should
just stay in the doorway
and nap.

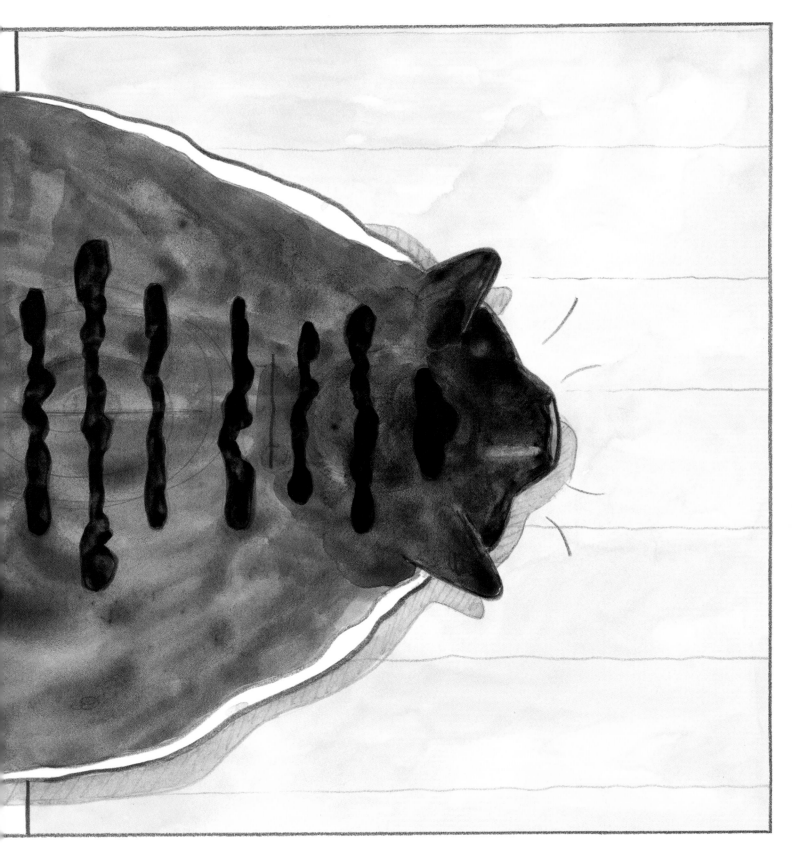

Of course, if he goes out he could meet other animals—

maybe he could chase the loons.

He'd hunt them
along the rock shore,

stalk them
through the reeds,

leap after them,
then eat them.

Maybe not.
Maybe somebody *else*
could chase the loons,
and he could watch.

But he's hungry.

Maybe he could catch a salmon.

The salmon would be so large,
he'd share it with some friendly bears.

He'd get to the bears' island
with the help of a moose.

He and the bears would pick
blueberries before dinner.

They would eat
salmon, and
blueberry pie.

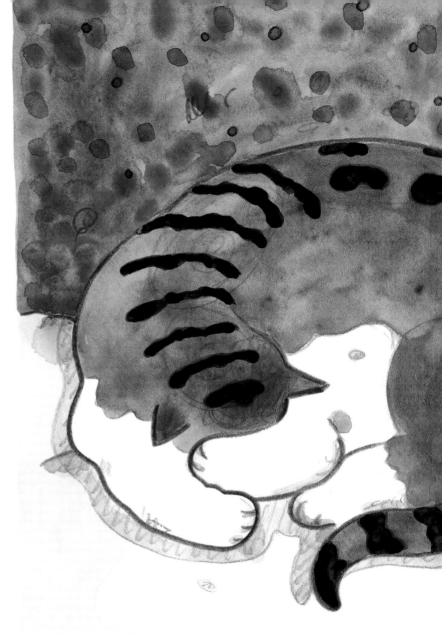

The bears
could clean up.

He would curl up
and close his eyes
and listen to the wind.

The world could pass him by.

And when he was ready, when the
shadows stretched across the lake,
maybe he'd ride the moose back home.

Maybe not.
Maybe, if he stays
right where he is,
Magic's next move
will come to him.